Fierce Milly
and the
Swizzled Eyes

Marilyn McLaughlin

Leonie Shearing

To John, who still believes

you can sneeze your eyes out

M.McL.

For H.B. and Charlie, my inspiration!

L.S.

First published in Great Britain 2002
by Egmont Books Ltd
239 Kensington High Street, London W8 6SA.
Text copyright © Marilyn McLaughlin 2002
Illustrations copyright © Leonie Shearing 2002
The author and illustrator have asserted their moral rights.
Paperback ISBN 0 7497 4808 7
10 9 8 7 6 5 4 3 2 1
A CIP catalogue record for this title is available from the British Library
Printed in Dubai

Contents

Red Bananas

No Pudding

Fierce Milly came round our house at teatime. Me and my wee brother Billy were just starting our puddings. It was our favourite – jam pudding.

'There's a ghost on the ceiling!' Fierce Milly yelled.

Where?

Me and Billy looked up. No ghost.

And when we looked down again – no
pudding.

A vanishing pudding!

'Hey, Susan!' Billy shouted. 'What
happened?'

'The ghost ate your puddings,' Fierce
Milly said.

'Fierce Milly ate our puddings,' I said.
'Look at all that jam on her face. That's
evidence. She must have hoovered up our
puddings without even using a spoon.'

'Oooooooh!' said Billy, disappointed. 'Does that mean there's no ghost?'

I was cross. 'It's not fair eating other people's puddings. Why can't you just be ordinary and not fierce?'

'Never! I'm Fierce Milly forever, and I eat all before me. Yesterday I ate twenty-seven babies.'

My tummy's as big as a bus and it's all full up.

'They were jelly babies,' I said quickly, before Billy would get the wrong idea. 'And they were mine. She was only supposed to take one.'

'Have my sardine sandwich instead,' she said. She might have been trying to look sorry but all I could see was jam.

'Yeuch!' I said. 'That sardine sandwich has been in your pocket since yesterday lunch-time. We're not speaking to you ever again.

Snap!

Cecil Nutt keep Out!

You're not our friend. Come on Billy.'

Me and Billy went and sat in the diggings.
The diggings is our secret den. Billy dug it,
and I'm in on the secret because I'm his big
sister. And Fierce Milly knows about it
because she's our best friend. And horrible
Cecil Nutt doesn't know about it at all
because he's our worst enemy.

You need two cards the same, Billy!

Fierce Milly came too, even though we weren't talking to her. She started to sing and dance around the diggings. Her singing is very loud with only one note. This was Fierce Milly's song:

'Susan's got no pudding,

Billy's got no pudding.

Gulp!

Gone!

Sulk huff!'

Sulky Susan!

Gulp!

Billy loves lists and he jumped
out of the diggings
and danced
around
shouting,

Slurp!

Burp!

'Guzzle, gulp,
gone,

Drool dribble,
slurp,

Gobble slobber,
BURP!'

'I'm going to close my eyes now,'
I announced in my see-if-I-care voice. 'I am
pretending that both of you are not there.'
I shut my eyes tight.

Billy said, 'But I'm still here Susan, I am.' And I knew he was feeling himself all over, just to be sure.

'It's good Susan has her eyes closed,' Fierce Milly said. 'She'll be all right if she sneezes.'

Since I was pretending she wasn't there as well as not talking to her, I couldn't just ask her what sneezing had to do with anything. I could only sit there with my eyes all screwed up, hoping that Billy would ask her.

Ask her Billy, please, please, PLEASE!

12

But I needn't have worried. Fierce Milly doesn't wait to be asked, not if she has something really good to tell you.

She said, 'If you sneeze with your eyes open, your eyeballs pop out!'

The Swizzled Eyes

Billy leapt into the diggings right on top of me and threw his two arms tight round my neck. My eyes popped open on their own, but did stay in.

'Susan, Susan, Susan!' Billy yelled. 'Can that happen?'

'Don't be silly. Your eyes are stuck in. Forever.'

'Well,' Fierce Milly said, 'It happened to me!'

Me and Billy turned round
slowly and looked at her. You can
look at someone even if you aren't
talking to them.

She sat down on the edge of the diggings.

Yo-yo Ferguson, next-
door's cat came and sat
down beside her as if he
wanted to hear the story
too. He was following her
about everywhere today.

15

'Last Saturday morning, I sneezed in my bedroom at half past ten. My eyes were open because I was looking at my new watch, and they popped right out. They flew all the way across the room, bounced off the wall and plopped down into my monster furry feet slippers.'

Sardines
mmm.

'Billy,' I said. 'Tell her, that if her eyes popped out and flew around the room, how did she know where they were going, when she wouldn't be able to see with them because they weren't connected up any more?' That would stump her.

'I could hear them whacking about,' said Fierce Milly.

'Susan,' whispered Billy. 'I need you to be talking to Fierce Milly again. This is *too* fierce.'

'When I put them back in again they were upside down, and I had to do cartwheels all the way down my front garden to swizzle them round the right way again. And now I've got special powers. I've got swizzled eyes,' Fierce Milly said.

'Susan . . .?' Billy pleaded.

Everything...

is...

upside...

down.

That's better!

'Oh, all right then, Billy. I'm talking
to her again, but it's only temporary.
How do you know you've got special
powers?' I asked.

'I stared out Yo-yo Ferguson. I took
control of his mind. He is my slave-cat
now and goes wherever I go. He is my
cat bodyguard.'

Yo-yo Ferguson was

Sardines?

rubbing his head against the pocket with the sardine sandwich in.

'Huummpf,' I said. 'He just wants your sardine sandwich.'

'And I stared myself out in the bathroom mirror and I cracked it right across.'

Hmmm . . . maybe.

That was true, there was a big crack right across Fierce Milly's bathroom mirror.

'And I stared out the statue in the park!'

That might be true.

'And last night, I stared out the moon!'

'Well, you'd definitely need special powers
for that!' I said.

Will she get us sweets?

'And now I'm going to stare out Tony in the corner shop. I'm going to take over his mind and make him give us all his sweets.'

'Can she be our friend again, Susan?' Billy asked.

She might.

'I don't see why not,' I said. 'But only if she promises not to swizzle us.'

Then I remembered. 'Fierce Milly, Tony banned you from the corner shop, for making up sweeties that don't exist, and asking for them all the time.'

'I'll make him forget I'm banned.'

Just watch me!

The Challenge

Fierce Milly went straight into Tony's shop, right up to the counter. Me and Billy waited in the doorway. Fierce Milly could just see over the top of the counter. She switched on her staring eyes. Stare, stare, stare.

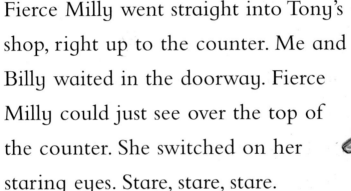

Tony didn't know she was there at first. Stare, stare, stare. Then he must have felt the stare and turned round, and he didn't say, 'Out, you're banned.' He said, 'And what can I do you for?'

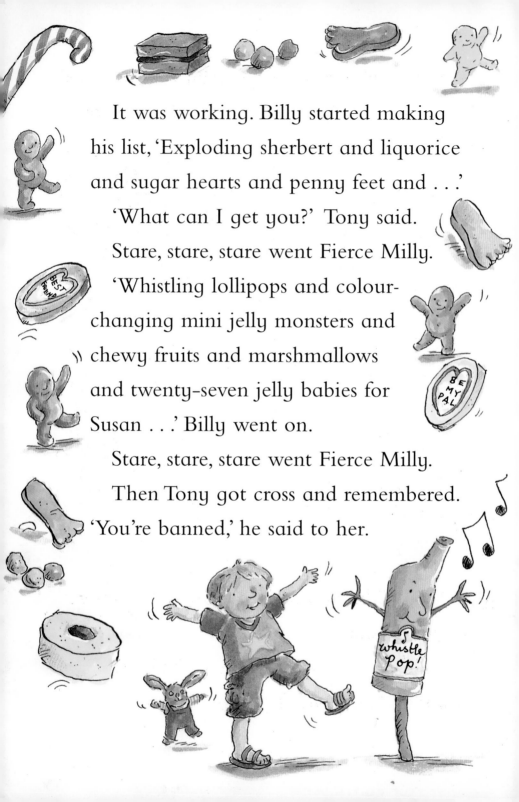

It was working. Billy started making his list, 'Exploding sherbert and liquorice and sugar hearts and penny feet and . . .'

'What can I get you?' Tony said.

Stare, stare, stare went Fierce Milly.

'Whistling lollipops and colour-changing mini jelly monsters and chewy fruits and marshmallows and twenty-seven jelly babies for Susan . . .' Billy went on.

Stare, stare, stare went Fierce Milly.

Then Tony got cross and remembered. 'You're banned,' he said to her.

'You're all banned. Especially Goggle Eyes. I don't know what she's up to, but she's not doing it in my shop.'

Out, Goggle Eyes!

'Why didn't it work?' Billy asked when we all got outside.

'I need more practice,' Fierce Milly said.

'I know! Cecil Nutt's granny!'

Cecil Nutt's house was just two doors away, and his granny was always asleep in her armchair just inside the front window.

'Come on Billy,' I yelled. 'This might be good.'

Fierce Milly said, 'When she wakes she'll be in my power and I'll make her keep Cecil Nutt in and give him porridge every day.'

She climbed right up on Cecil Nutt's front windowsill and pressed her face against the glass. Yo-yo Ferguson jumped up beside her.

Nothing happened.

Then Cecil Nutt came up

the street and yelled,

'Oy, what are you doing?'

We all yelled and Fierce Milly

jumped down and Yo-yo

Ferguson ran off.

Some bodyguard

he turned out to be.

'It wasn't me,' Fierce Milly said. But there was a big jammy face print on the window pane, and there was only one of us with a jammy face. Billy tried to make it better.

'She was only trying to stare out your granny. She's got swizzled eyes. She's got special powers. She can stare out the moon.'

'Bet she can't stare out me,' roared Cecil Nutt.

'Bet I can,' roared Fierce Milly.

Then all the shouting woke up Cecil Nutt's
granny and she came storming out, grabbed
him by the back of his t-shirt and whisked
him into the house. He had time to yell,
'Tomorrow at breaktime! Stare you out!'
before the door banged shut.

'To the death!' Fierce Milly yelled in through the letterbox. Nobody had ever stared out Cecil Nutt before, but Fierce Milly wasn't one bit worried. 'See? It was me made her take him in. And she's probably giving him porridge for supper, right now.'

Enjoy your porridge!

The Big Stare

Fierce Milly came to school the next day in sunglasses. To protect us from her special powers she said. But Miss made her take them off. Everybody was talking about the Big Stare and at breaktime we all made a circle round Cecil Nutt and Fierce Milly.

'When I win,' Fierce Milly said, 'you will be my slave and do everything I tell you forever.'

Everybody cheered because that sounded great. Nobody likes Cecil Nutt.

'When I win,' Cecil Nutt said, 'you will not be Fierce Milly anymore. You will just be Milly.'

Everybody gasped, because that would be terrible.

The Big Stare began. Nobody spoke.

Nobody moved. Cecil Nutt and Fierce Milly
stared and stared and stared. Big Stares take
a long time. It got boring, and more boring.

Some people went off to play football.
Some people went off to play wrestling and
some people went off to play Pop Stars.

It's taking ages.

Sshh!

Me and Billy stayed because we're Fierce Milly's best friends. We hardly dared breathe.

Fierce Milly and Cecil Nutt were just a nose length apart, staring, staring, staring.

Billy whispered, 'What if one of them sneezes?'

Stare Stare Stare

Break's over.

Then Miss came out to ring
the bell for the end of break, and
fell over.

Everybody yelled and Fierce
Milly looked around to see what
was happening and Cecil Nutt won.

35

Miss fell over because she tripped on Yo-yo Ferguson. Cats aren't allowed in school, so everybody tried to catch Yo-yo Ferguson. He belted right across the tarmac and up the big tree by the gate.

Then everybody ran all the way back over the playground to see if Miss was knocked out or anything interesting like that.

I won! I won!

Miss fell down!

Oh dear me!

Help!

But she only had two sore knees and wasn't even crying. She put her special blue dinosaur plasters on the sore places, so we spent the whole afternoon watching the plasters on Miss's knees and nobody remembered about Fierce Milly losing the Big Stare.

I'll be doctor!

Is it bleeding?

No me!

Except for Fierce Milly. She was quiet all the way home.

I'm away home.

'Are your eyes still swizzled?' asked Billy.

'You can still be Fierce to us,' I said.

'I'm going home to get changed,' she said.

'We'll call for you after,' I said. And we did, and got an awful shock. She wasn't fierce anymore!

She was ordinary! Her face was clean, her hair was brushed, and she was wearing white frilly ankle socks.

'Come on, let's go and play,' I said.

'I can't come and play with you,' she said, 'because I don't want to get my white frilly ankle socks dirty from sitting in the diggings.'

Then she closed the front door and went back in. Me and Billy shouted in through the letterbox, 'Come on, Fierce Milly, play with us!'

But all that happened was that we heard her say, 'It's rude to shout in people's letterboxes,' and then nothing.

The Frilly White Socks

Sitting in the diggings was no fun
without Fierce Milly. We had to get her
out of those frilly ankle socks. We had to
get her Fierce again.

'We've got to think of something,' I
said.

These were Billy's ideas: 'Steal the
frilly white ankle socks. Stick up Cecil
Nutt's front door with superglue so that
he can't get out to call her Milly. Get
Fierce Milly earplugs . . .'

Then Mr Ferguson shouted over the
hedge, 'Have any of you seen my cat? He
hasn't come home.'

Me and Billy
went to look for
Yo-yo Ferguson.
We looked under cars
and we looked in wheelie bins.

We looked in Tony's shop but he only
shouted, 'OUT!'

Then Billy remembered where
he'd last seen Yo-yo Ferguson.
Up the tree at the school gate.

We went to see, and sure enough, there was Yo-yo Ferguson, right at the top of the tree, mewing loudly.

'He wants his tea,' Billy said.

'Let's go and get Fierce Milly,' I said, 'she'll know what to do, even if she's not fierce any more.'

Fierce Milly knew an emergency when she heard of one. She dashed straight out of the house, frilly white ankle socks and all.

We ran off to have a look at Yo-yo
Ferguson stuck up the school tree.

Yo-yo Ferguson looked down.

We looked up, and that's how we didn't see
Cecil Nutt arrive.

'Look who it is,' he said. 'Little Milly in her
frilly socks, Frilly Milly. Frilleeeee Milleeeeeee.'

Little Milly frowned hugely, and suddenly
looked like her usual self.

'Bet I can get that cat down from the tree
before you,' she said.

'Bet I can do it first,' Cecil Nutt said.

'And if I get the cat down first, I'll be fierce
again. I'll be Fierce Milly forever.'

'Okay,' said Cecil Nutt and he jumped up into the tree and got stuck three branches up. He threw his arms and legs around the tree and hugged it tight.

'I'm going to fall. I'm up too high,' he yelled. 'I'm stuck.'

Fierce Milly took something from her pocket. It was a sardine sandwich. Yo-yo Ferguson came down the tree fast.

Sardines, at last!

He ran right over the top of stuck Cecil Nutt, jumped down, grabbed the sardine sandwich and ran off home.

Fierce Milly shouted up at Cecil Nutt, 'What do you call me now?'

Help!

'Fierce Milly! Get help, Fierce Milly! Don't leave me up here, please, Fierce Milly!'

'Maybe I'll ring the fire brigade, maybe I won't. Who knows?' Fierce Milly said.

Fierce Milly!

We told his dad about him being stuck up the tree, and his dad got a ladder and rescued him and made him say, 'Thank you, Fierce Milly,' and then he sent him to bed early to remind him to stay out of trees.

Fierce Milly said she knew a really good place for frogspawn, so we went off to get some. It was great. She got all dirty and her hair got messed up and we brought the frogspawn home in her frilly white socks.

Her mum sighed, 'Still, at least she's lost that strange staring look. I was beginning to think she needed spectacles.'